A Wilcox and Griswold Mystery

THE CASE
OF THE
BAD APPLES

BY
ROBIN NEWMAN

ILLUSTRATED BY
DEBORAH ZEMKE

Boys and girls, this case is about some bad apples on Ed's farm.

Over 100 animals live on this farm. Most work. Some horse around. Others steal.

That's where I come in. My name is Detective Wilcox. I'm a policemouse.

The boss is Captain Griswold. We're MFIs, Missing Food Investigators. It's our job to investigate cases of missing food. But strangely, in this particular case, food appeared where it wasn't expected!

Whatever the food, whatever the crime, we make the bad guys do the time.

****

It was seven o'clock Wednesday morning. The captain and I were finishing the paperwork on a poached egg case when the phone rang.

Case File #92959:
The Bad Apples

7:00 am, Headquarters

"MFI. Wilcox, here."

"This is Dr. Alberta Einswine from Whole Hog Emergency Care."

"What's up, Doc?"

"I've got an interesting case.

I think Porcini might have been poisoned."

"Poisoned?" I asked. "What happened?"

"This morning he found a gift basket of apples in front of his pen. Naturally, he pigged out."

"Well, he IS a pig."

2

"He wolfed down most of the apples — cores, seeds, and part of the basket, too! Then he got sick as a dog. Thing is he's not a dog. A pig like him shouldn't have gotten sick from eating apples. Lucky for him, an anonymous squealer called SWINE-1-1 for help."

"Did you run a tox screen?"

"I'm off to do that now," said Dr. Einswine. "Porcini is still green around the gills, but stable and resting in his pen. I hope the MFI can get some answers."

TOX SCREEN: That's police talk for a test that checks for the presence of poisons.

"We're on it! Captain, we've got a Code 22, attempted hamslaughter."

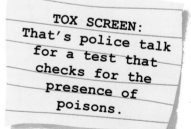

We hopped in the cruiser and the captain turned on the siren. Rush hour traffic was heavy: road hogs. There was squealing, oinking, and grunting, but they finally let us pass. Typical road hogs. Typical indeed.

The Crime Scene

7:20 am, Porcini's Pen

"Detectives, you've got to save my bacon!" squealed Porcini.

"Give me the facts and just the facts," I said, pulling out my notepad and pen.

"Right after Colonel Peck crowed, my scent-sa-tional snout picked up the smell of delicious apples."

"Aren't Delicious apples red?" I asked, pointing to a chewed-up green apple on the ground.

"Oh! I didn't mean *Red Delicious* apples. I meant delicious as in *YUMMY*! My snout led me straight to this basket of apples."

"What did you do then?"

"I went hog wild and made a pig of myself. Wouldn't you?"

The captain flashed me his "no-way-I'm-a-mouse" look.

"Everyone knows an apple a day keeps the doctor away. I figured I'd be as healthy as an ox if I ate the whole basket. Instead, my tummy hurts."

"Any idea who left the apples and why?" I asked.

"Everyone's been mad because I beefed up pen security."

"Everyone?" I questioned. "Who's everyone?"

"Sweet Pea, the new piglet next door, Herman the Vermin, that dirty rat, and Hot Dog. They've all been sneaking into my pen and stealing my food!" oinked Porcini. "Look at me! I'm skinnier than a string bean."

I looked. Porcini was a little green but he didn't look anything like a string bean.

"I had to do something. First I locked the door between my pen and Sweet Pea's. Next, I covered the holes Herman had dug. Then I put in an alarm that rang whenever Hot Dog or anyone else was poking around my slop."

"What about video cameras?" I asked. A video might have picked up an image of the perp.

PERP: That's the bad guy who committed the crime.

"I guess I should have installed those, too. Owie! My tummy hurts!" Porcini groaned.

"Anyone who might have seen who left the basket?" I asked.

"Check with Sweet Pea next door."

The captain inspected the basket. It could easily hold half a bushel of apples, about 34 medium-sized apples. With the bow on the handle, it looked like a gift. But who was it from?

Four apples were left. The captain's whiskers twitched. I knew what that meant: Granny Smith apples for sure. These items were evidence. They needed to be labeled and bagged carefully.

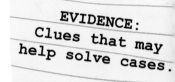

EVIDENCE: Clues that may help solve cases.

The captain taped off the crime scene and dusted for prints while I took photographs.

"Captain, did you see this? Hoof, claw, and paw prints."

I did a quick sketch in my notepad showing the location and direction of the prints.

"Thanks, Porcini. We have what we need for now." I shut my notepad. "Feel better."

We made a quick stop at headquarters to drop off the evidence at the forensics lab. Then it was time to grill the suspects.

FORENSICS LAB: A place where evidence is examined.

"Captain," I said, "if Porcini was poisoned, some rotten apple went to a lot of trouble to get rid of him."

Some rotten apple indeed.

Chapter 3

Suspects & Clues

Suspect #1

SWEET PEA

8:15 am, Sweet Pea's Pen

Knock. Knock. The captain rapped on the gate.

"Do I smell cheese donuts?" squealed a piglet.

The captain forked one over.

"Are you Sweet Pea?" I asked.

"That's me! Sweetest little pea in the pen," she said, batting her eyelashes.

This piglet was a ham.

"Captain Griswold and Detective Wilcox, MFIs." I flashed my badge. "Porcini got a gift basket of apples, but it wasn't much of a present. Those apples might have been poisoned."

"The apples were poi-poi-poi-soned?"

"Did you suspect they were poisoned?" I gave Sweet Pea the third degree.

"N-n-n-o, sir."

"Did you leave the poisoned apples for Porcini?"

"N-n-n-o, sir," she said. "I wouldn't hurt a fly!"

"Did you see who left the basket?"

Sweet Pea swore she had been home all last night and this morning and hadn't seen any-one dropping off the apples or hanging around the pen.

A check of the MFI database showed the piglet's record was as squeaky clean as her spotless pen. The captain flashed me his "her-pen-might-be-too-clean" look. I had to agree. Not one crumb was out of place. There was no sign of apples or poison.

The only things that stood out were a copy of *Snow White* and a blanket on her bed, stitched with the words, *Love, Granny*.

"What a beautiful blanket!" I said.

I couldn't put my toe on it, but there was definitely something familiar about the blanket.

Sweet Pea quickly hugged it to her chest. "It was a gift from my Granny Hammy."

The captain handed Sweet Pea a card with the MFI hotline number.

"If you remember anything, give us a ring," I told her.

The captain and I hopped in the cruiser. Time we had a word with Herman, the rat. Frankly, this case was inching along at a snail's pace. At a snail's pace indeed.

8:50 am, Herman's Rusty Old Truck
The captain pounded on the door.

"Scram!" came a voice from inside the truck.

"I smell a rat!" I whispered to the captain. "Herman, open up! MFIs."

The truck window rolled down. "What do you want? I don't have time for ratfinks."

"We heard about your beef with Porcini."

"That no good, pig-headed pig covered every hole I dug. The nerve! How am I supposed to steal his food now?"

"Is that why you tried to poison him?"

"Me? Poison Porcini? Ha! I'd never waste good pork chops."

When I asked Herman if he knew anything about the apples left in front of Porcini's pen, he denied it.

"Where were you last night?" I probed.

"Trying to see if I have an alibi?"

The scowl on the captain's face read, "answer-the-question-before-I-haul-your-tail-down-to-headquarters."

"I went to the garbage dump. A rat's got to eat. And that's when everything went from the frying pan right into the fire."

"What do you mean?" I asked.

"While I was scrounging for snacks, Fowler, the owl, grabbed me."

"How did you get away?"

"Hot Dog threw something at Fowler. Bulls-eye! Got her right in the talons. She dropped me like a hot potato."

"What did Hot Dog throw?"

"Something round, like an apple."

I glanced over at the captain. He gave me his "an-apple-like-the-ones-in-the-basket" look.

Herman caught the look. He narrowed his eyes. "Hey, you two aren't trying to get me to rat on Hot Dog, are you?"

"What color apple did Hot Dog throw?" I pressed, hoping Herman would spill the beans.

Herman shrugged. "Once Fowler dropped me, I hightailed it out of there. Apple, shmapple."

"Where were you this morning?"

"Back at the dump. It was slim pickings, but on my way home I passed Hot Dog practicing yoga with the goats."

Hmm. . . if Herman's story checked out, Hot Dog would have an alibi.

"Mind if we look inside your truck?"

"You better have a warrant or it'll cost you a couple of cheese donuts."

WARRANT:
A legal document that gives police the right to make an arrest or search a place.

We didn't have a warrant, so the captain tossed him the donuts. We scoured the truck. What a rat's nest! Potato peels were everywhere, but no apples and no poison.

"Herman, we're done. Don't scamper out of town any time soon."

The captain and I jumped into the cruiser and made a quick stop at Fowler's. She confirmed Herman's story. The rat's alibi was solid.

Next up was Hot Dog. He had some explaining to do about that possible assault with an apple. He might very well be in the dog house. In the dog house indeed.

ASSAULT:
An attack.

10:10 am, Hot Dog's House

BONK! An apple almost hit the captain on the head. He flashed me his "Hot-Dog-is-up-a-tree" look.

"Up a tree indeed!" I said. "Hot Dog, got a minute?"

"Sure thing, detectives. Want an apple? They're delicious."

Hot Dog was right. They were Delicious apples. *Red Delicious* apples. The captain shook his head. The crime scene apples were green.

"Might as well be apples and oranges," I grumbled. "Say, Hot Dog, we heard you left Porcini's in a stew yesterday."

"Porcini said I swiped his slop — which I didn't — and banned me from his pen. Why are you asking?"

"Did you poison Porcini?" I asked.

"Poison Porcini?! You're barking up the wrong tree. Go ask Sweet Pea or Herman. They were kicked out, too. And I heard Herman was madder than a wet hen."

"Right now we're talking to you. Where were you last night?"

Hot Dog repeated Herman's story that he had saved the rat from Fowler.

"What about this morning?"

"I was doing Downward Dog at yoga class."

Hot Dog gave us permission to search his doghouse. There were dog biscuits everywhere but no sign of anything incriminating.

Then the captain spotted something under Hot Dog's bed.

The something was ROUND and GREEN. The captain scurried underneath and pushed out...

"Hey, thanks! I was looking for my tennis ball!" woofed Hot Dog.

We drove back to headquarters. From my desk, I called the goat shed. Yogi the Goatee picked up.

"Ohhhhhmmmmm."

"Detective Wilcox here. Was Hot Dog at your yoga class this morning?"

"Ohhhhmmmmm."

That was yoga for yes. Hot Dog's alibi was airtight. We were scraping the bottom of the apple barrel, that's for sure! Bottom of the apple barrel indeed.

Chapter 4

Forensics

12:02 pm, Headquarters

The captain and I took the elevator down to the forensics lab.

"Detectives, come look at this," said Dr. Phil.

"There are two sets of hoof prints on all four apples left at the scene. I checked the database and the prints marked A are an exact match for Porcini. The prints marked B are similar to Porcini's but smaller. I couldn't find a match for them in our database."

"But they're pig prints?" I asked.

"Definitely! All of the saliva samples on the chewed apples were a match for Porcini so he was the only one who ate anything."

"No surprise there," I said.

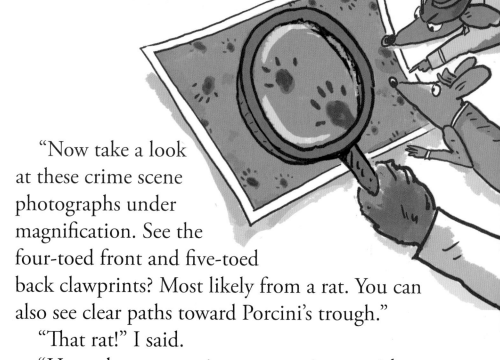

"Now take a look at these crime scene photographs under magnification. See the four-toed front and five-toed back clawprints? Most likely from a rat. You can also see clear paths toward Porcini's trough."

"That rat!" I said.

"Here, these paw prints are consistent with that of a dog. They have a roundish shape and blunt claw marks. There isn't a straight trail, though."

"That low-down dog! Can you identify the rat and dog?" I asked.

"Unfortunately, there's not enough here to make a positive ID. Strangest thing was that there was no trace of any kind of poison."

Who could have poisoned Porcini without any poison? Think. Think. Think. I tossed the captain and Dr. Phil some cheese donuts. We were all pacing. One, two, three steps forward. One, two, three steps backwards.

I pulled out my notepad and looked at my sketch of the crime scene. "Holy baked apples!"

Just then the phone rang.
"Wilcox here, MFI."
"This is Dr. Einswine. Meet me at Porcini's pen. I've got his test results."
"We're on our way!"
Time we found out who had upset the apple cart. Upset the apple cart indeed.

Chapter 5

Hogs and Kisses

1:05 pm, In front of the pigpens

Dr. Alberta Einswine was trotting up just as we got there. Sweet Pea was there, too.

"Porcini, you may want to sit down," said Dr. Einswine. "I have the results of your tox screen."

"Is it bad news?" he asked.

"I'm afraid..." she started to say.

"How much time do I have? Days? Hours?"
He choked up. "Minutes?"

"Your tox screen showed high levels of..."
Porcini looked scared, but it was Sweet Pea who
was sweating like a pig.

"Cyanide."

"Not cyanide!" wheezed Porcini.

"Not cyanide!" gasped Sweet Pea.

"What's cyanide?" asked Porcini.

"Poison."

"I was POI-POI-POISONED!!!"
Porcini turned lime green, his knees buckled...

and he fainted.

"He was poi-poi-poi-soned!" said Sweet Pea.
She turned pea green,
her knees buckled,
and she fainted.

The captain placed a damp cloth on Sweet Pea's brow while Dr. Einswine told Porcini to take deep, slow breaths.

"It's time to fess up Sweet Pea," I said.

"I'm s-s-s-sorry," blubbered Sweet Pea as she came to. "I never meant to hurt Porcini."

"It was YOU?" oinked Porcini.

"You were so sad. I just wanted to cheer you up with a basket of Granny Smith apples. Cross my hooves, I didn't poi-poi-poison anything!"

"Well, if you didn't poison me, then who did? Was it Herman? Or Hot Dog?"

"It wasn't Herman or Hot Dog," I said.

"Well, it had to be SOMEBODY!" snorted Porcini.

"WHO?!"

Dr. Einswine took a deep breath. "It was...**_YOU!_**"

"ME? I poisoned MYSELF?"

Porcini turned the color of a bright red Delicious apple. "That's completely

PIG-DIC-U-LOUS!

"Do the math," said Dr. Einswine. "You ate around 30 apples. Assuming an average of five seeds per apple, by my calculations, that's 150 seeds. Each apple seed contains amygdalin, which becomes cyanide when chewed and digested. Eating so many apple seeds is what poisoned you. Stop eating apple seeds and you should feel better soon."

Porcini was so relieved he gave Sweet Pea a whole hog and kiss.

"Detectives, I'm sorry," said Sweet Pea. "I should have told you the truth, but I was scared you'd think I poisoned Porcini. How did you know the apples were from me?"

"It was the second set of hoof prints found on the apples. They were like Porcini's, but smaller. Those same hoof prints were found in the mud near the basket. You're the only pig on the farm with hooves that size.

"And then there was your blanket."

"My blanket?"

"At first I thought Granny referred to Granny Hammy but in fact, doesn't it say Granny Smith?"

Sweet Pea spread out her blanket for everyone to see. "Granny Hammy made my blanket from a Granny Smith apple sack."

"Did I hear my name?"

"Granny Hammy!" squealed Sweet Pea.

"Detectives, I promise I'll never eat another apple again," oinked Porcini. "From now on, apples are forbidden fruit!"

"What about my fresh baked apple pie?" asked Granny Hammy. "Hot out of the oven!"

"Perhaps I could make a small exception," oinked Porcini. "I'd hate to be rude."

News of fresh baked apple pie travelled faster than two shakes of a lamb's tail.

The captain tossed me an apple. "Thanks!" I said, taking a bite. "Captain, maybe there's some truth to the saying, '*An apple a day keeps the doctor away.*' **An** apple a day indeed."

3:00 pm, Case closed.

Food for Thought

It is true that pigging out on apple seeds can make you sick. Apple seeds contain amygdalin, which releases small amounts of cyanide when it's chewed and comes into contact with digestive enzymes. But you would have to chew LOTS of apple seeds to actually get sick. So, have your apple a day, and if you accidentally eat a few apple seeds, do not worry. They are safe to eat in small quantities.

Boys and girls, the case you just read was about some bad apples that turned out to be pretty good after all.

Every day there's a food problem on the farm. Sometimes it's missing or lost. Sometimes it's stolen. Sometimes it's just applesauce.

With all these animals you can be sure of one thing: trouble. It only takes one bad apple to spoil the bunch.

Whatever the food, whatever the crime, MFIs make the bad guys do the time.

Mollie Katzen's
Apple Pockets Recipe

Have a grown-up help you with this recipe.

Ingredients:
- 1 1/4 cups lukewarm water
- 1 tsp yeast
- 3 tbsp sugar
- 3 tbsp butter
- 3 cups all-purpose flour

- 1 1/4 tsp salt
- 1 1/2 tsp cornstarch
- 1/4 tsp cinnamon
- 2 tart apples, peeled, cored, and quartered

First make basic yeast dough:
1. Combine lukewarm water, yeast and 1 tbsp of the sugar in a small bowl.
2. Melt 2 tbsp butter in a small bowl (~30 seconds in the microwave should do it).
3. Measure out 1 tbsp of melted butter and add to bowl of yeasty water, saving rest of butter for later.
4. Combine flour and salt in a food processsor. As it runs, pour water mixture in slowly. Mix well for a few seconds.
5. Tip the dough out of food processor onto a well-floured board and knead, pushing it with floury hands for around 2-3 minutes.
6. Put ball of dough into bowl with the remaining butter. Swish dough around to coat in butter, then turn it upside-down and leave covered to rise for an hour.
7. After an hour, dough is ready to use. Cut in half and freeze half for later. Use the other half for Apple Pockets now!

Make the Apple Pockets:
8. Preheat oven to 400 degrees. Spray a baking tray with oil or rub with soft butter.
9. In a small bowl combine cornstarch, 5 tsp sugar, and cinnamon. Mix well.
10. Sprinkle cornstarch mixture into a mixing bowl with peeled apple chunks and stir gently with wooden spoon until apples are completely coated.
11. Sprinkle flour onto a board and divide dough into 4 balls on it.
12. Using flour on your hands and the rolling pin, roll out each ball into a circle 6-7 inches wide.
13. Melt the remaining 1 tbsp of butter in the microwave.
14. Brush some melted butter onto each circle of dough, then divide apples into four parts and arrange apple mixture onto one-half of each circle.
15. Fold the other side of the circle over and press edges together with a fork.
16. Put pockets on the oiled baking tray, lightly spray with water, and sprinkle the tops with 1/2 teaspoon sugar.
17. Bake for 25 minutes at 400 degrees, take out and let cool for 15 minutes.
18. Eat!

Mollie Katzen generously provided this recipe. You can find it and others like it in her children's cookbook, *Honest Pretzels*.